I0738463

2018 Storytellers Award Winner

Hearts at War

Storytellers Award Winner 2018

HEARTS at WAR

Rob Winblad

Illustrated by Zechariah Olson

Visit S.C. TreeHouse Press' website at press.sctreehouse.com

Find more works for creators at storytellers.sctreehouse.com

S.C.TREEHOUSE and S.C. TreeHouse's logo are registered trademarks of S.C. TreeHouse LLC.

S.C.TREEHOUSE PRESS and S.C. TreeHouse Press' logo are registered trademarks of S.C. TreeHouse LLC.

STORYTELLERS and Storytellers' logo are registered trademarks of S.C. TreeHouse LLC.

Hearts at War

Copyright © 2018 by Nightwalker Scrolls. All rights reserved.

Cover illustration copyright © 2019 Christopher D. Stewart. All rights reserved.

Designed by Zechariah Olson and Christopher D. Stewart

Edited by Kimberly Winblad, Marvin Hangguard, and Christopher D. Stewart

Published in association with Storytellers a protected series of S.C. TreeHouse LLC and S.C. TreeHouse Press a protected series of S.C. TreeHouse LLC and Nightwalker Scrolls.

This novel is a work of fiction. Names, characters, businesses, places, events, locales, and incidents are either the products of the author's imagination or used in a fictitious manner. Any resemblance to actual persons, living or dead, or actual events is purely coincidental and beyond the intent of either the author of publisher.

All rights reserved. No part of this book may be reproduced or transmitted in any form or by any means, electronic or mechanical, including photocopying, recording, or by an information storage and retrieval system - except by a reviewer who may quote brief passages in a review to be printed in a magazine or newspaper - without permission in writing from the publisher.

Printed in the United State of America

A short story about forgiveness and love.

Prologue

Good-byes,

Love, and War

May 13th, Nineteen Sixty-Six:

Lieutenant Carl Daniels felt as if he was going to explode from the conflicting emotions that he was experiencing. On the one hand, he was absolutely euphoric: Rhiannon Jacobs had said yes,

and they had just been married. On the other hand, he felt a strange mixture of regret and excitement at the reason for their rather hurried wedding: He was shipping out for Vietnam with his unit in two days. On the other hand, he reasoned, she had known that his unit was on ready notice for deployment when they met at the dance, and she had said yes, a few weeks later anyway, so she had known pretty much what she was getting in to. On the other hand, the recent reports had mentioned some pretty heavy fighting, and his unit was going into the thick of it; not to mention the fact that they hadn't had much more than a total of six or seven weeks together. On the other hand, he had four fingers and a thumb. Shaking his head to clear the crazy tangle of thoughts chasing each other in circles, he turned from the rail of the ferry taking them to Liberty Island, he smiled down at Rhiannon, his right arm tightening around her. "I'm glad we could make it to see the Statue of Liberty. This will be fun; you'll see."

Rhiannon smiled back. "Yeah. I just hope the lines aren't too long; I'd like to actually get inside, see what the view is like from up there."

Glancing ahead, Carl clenched his jaw at the sight of a clump of anti-war protestors waving placards smeared with scrawls like 'Get out of Vietnam,' 'Make Love, not War', and 'Bring back our boys.' As he stepped off the ferry, he wondered if it had been a wise move to wear his uniform on the sightseeing tour he had planned with Rhiannon; but he was proud of his country, he had volunteered for the Army, and he didn't care what these pot-headed hooligans thought about it. Pushing past a placard-waving man in rumpled slacks and shirt, no tie, his jacket folded up on a bench nearby, Carl guided Rhiannon to the line for the public-access door to the Statue of Liberty. Fortunately, the line was short, which for Carl was a good thing in more ways than one: the looks he was getting from the protestors were getting uglier, and a confrontation seemed imminent if he didn't get out of their sight. Climbing the steps to the top, he stared out across the harbor in awe, forgetting for the moment his unease with heights. It was not quite to a fear, and he would dispute the claims of anyone who tried to say that it was a fear, but he had a healthy respect for gravity and its effects on things that were not designed to fly, so he preferred to remain closer to the ground in case he was suddenly compelled to obey the law of gravity in a precipitous manner. Finally, they headed back down the endless stairs, back across the ferry, and down a small side street to a downstairs Italian restaurant, he had found as a teenager growing up in Manhattan. As the waiter re-treated with their orders, Carl reached across the table and clasped Rhiannon's hand in his own. "Penny for your thoughts."

Rhiannon smiled. "I thought that was *my* line."

Carl shrugged. "I guess I just kicked that cliche to the curb. So, what's on your mind?"

Rhiannon directed her gaze at the flickering flame of the candle stuck in the bottle between them on the worn red-and-white checkered tablecloth. "I dunno. I guess… I guess it's wherever it is you're goin'."

Fighting back a stab of regret as he thought of his impending departure, Carl gently squeezed her hand. "Don't think of me there. Think of me here, with you. We've got two more days; so let's fill 'em with everything you ever wanted to do."

He patted his jacket pocket, where he kept a photo of her. "And even when I'm gone, I'll carry a piece of you with me, and you'll always have a piece of me here, with you, in your heart. Forever."

Rhiannon smiled, her eyes luminescent in the candlelight. Carl stared at her face, imprinting the memory of it in his mind so that he would always remember her this way. Twining her fingers in his, she touched their rings together. "Forever."

Chapter 1

A New Story

Forty Years Later:

Sergeant Rick Newman of Third Platoon, Delta Company, 2nd Combat Engineer Battalion, 2nd Marines, drew a deep breath as he stepped out of his car, staring at the old cafe he had worked at for the last five years. Walking in, he smiled a

greeting at the waitress. "Good morning Annie. Is Leslie in?"

With a smile, Annie nodded. "Yes, she's in the back. I'll go get her."

A moment later, a willowy young woman with long strawberry-blond hair and a light dusting of freckles on the bridge of her nose came running out of the back. "Rick!"

Sweeping her up in his arms, Rick spun her around once before setting her down. "Oh, goodness it's great to see you!"

As they sat down in the break room, Leslie ran a finger along the stripes on his sleeve. "You made Sergeant. Congratulations."

With a smile, Rick nodded. "Yeah, I'll bet that will impress your dad even more, huh?"

Giggling, Leslie punched him in the arm. "You don't need stripes to impress my dad, and you know it! So how long are you on furlough for?"

Rick lost some of his smile. "Unfortunately, only three days. Then my unit is shipping out for Africa. They've been dealing with a lot of difficulty with the humanitarian operation we're overrunning over there, and they need more Engineers, so we're shipping out as soon as possible."

Leslie's smile followed suit. "Oh. I was hoping it would be a little longer. Oh, well, at least it isn't someplace really dangerous."

Rick nodded. "Yes, and your brother is coming along."

Leslie brightened. "Oh, you and Harry got in the same unit? Great!"

Rick turned as the door to the break room opened to reveal a short, thinly built man with short-cropped red hair and a big grin on his face, wearing a uniform virtually identical to Rick's. "Hey Sis; good to see you and Rick are still getting along."

Bouncing up out of her seat, Leslie ran over to give him a hug. "Hi, Harry! How have you been?"

Harry shrugged, ambling over to the table. "Oh, pretty good. I only made Corporal, though, so clearly Rick did better than I did."

His grin belying any possible resentment in the words, he continued. "Anyway, we both got into the same platoon, and so far, we're working in the same breaching team."

Leslie smiled. "Well, that sounds like fun."

Rick smirked. "Yes. 'Join the Marine Engineers. Travel to exotic, foreign countries, see amazing architecture, meet exciting people, and then kill them, blow up their architecture, and build your own on the ruins.' Makes a nice recruiting slogan, but I kinda doubt they would want to use it."

Further conversation was interrupted as a tall, heavily built man with gray-streaked red hair and glasses walked into the break room. "All right then, lassie, break's over. Ricky, lad, good to see you! Come back to get your old job back?"

Smiling, Rick shook the man's extended hand. "Not this time, unfortunately, Mr. O'Dooley. I just got a three-day furlough before shipping out for Africa, and I decided to come say goodbye to everyone here while I had the chance."

Sam O'Dooley smiled. "And by 'everyone,' you, of course, meant Miss Nichols here."

Rick blushed. "Well, I'm saying goodbye to you, aren't I? And I was going to say goodbye to Annie on the way out, too. Yeah, and my next stop is Mr. Wakowski over at the construction company, and Mr. Feldman over at the auto body shop, and, well, there are some other people on my list, okay?"

Sam nodded sagely. "Oh, of course, of course. If you say so, lad."

Giving Leslie another hug, Rick shook hands with Sam and then left, stopping by Annie's post. "Goodbye, Annie. I'm shipping out in a couple of days."

With a grin, Annie gave him a quick hug. "Goodbye then, Rick. Me and Da are going to miss you."

Driving over to the construction company, Rick smiled a greeting at the receptionist, a short, round-faced woman a few years older than him. "Good afternoon, Trudy, I was hoping to see Mr. Wakowski, if he's free. I'm shipping out in a few days, so I was hoping to say goodbye."

Nodding, Trudy smiled as she hit the intercom. "Mr. Wakowski, Rick Newman is here to see you."

"All right, Trudy, send him in."

Anton Wakowski, a tall, thin descendant of Polish immigrants, stood to offer his hand as Rick walked in. "Hi, Rick, good to see you again! How are the Marines treating you?"

Rick smiled as he seated himself. "Pretty good; unfortunately, my unit is shipping out for Africa in a few days, so I dropped by to say goodbye. I also want to thank you for letting me work part-time here when I could; it's been really fun learning some of the tricks of the trade and applying some of the stuff that I've been learning in Engineers."

As Mr. Wakowski looked surprised, Rick nodded. "Oh, yeah, one of the selling points that recruiters use is that if you go for the Engineers, you learn skills that you can apply in the civilian construction market."

Mr. Wakowski looked impressed. "Wow. Well, when you get out, if you want a job here, you've got one, Rick. Stay safe over there; don't drink the water, don't eat anything funny, and stay away from the local wildlife and people." Rising to his feet, he extended his hand. "Good luck."

Rob Winblad

Chapter 2

Safe Travels

Stowing his duffel in the overhead compartment, Rick settled into the aisle seat, staring out at the bustling airport. Many of the passengers were in uniform; both Bravo and Delta Companies of the 2nd Light Armored Reconnaissance Battalion, the Black Knights and Outlaws, respectively, were shipping out on this set of flights in addition to nearly the entire Combat Engineers

Battalion. Looking up as someone tapped him on the shoulder, he shot to his feet and saluted hastily, recognizing the Lieutenant's bars on the newcomer. Casually returning the salute, the Lieutenant moved past him and plopped into the window seat before grabbing a magazine from the seat back and flipping it open as he waited for the remaining passengers to board.

After the safety procedures had been gone through, and the plane had taken off, Rick began his anti-jet lag/anti-deep-vein-thrombosis measures. Downing a bottle of water from the drink cart, he set his watch alarm for two hours, slid a pair of complimentary headphones over his ears and turned on his iTunes library as he closed his eyes. It felt like he had just dropped off when his alarm chimed at him, and he opened his eyes, getting up and pacing the length of the aisle. As he returned from the fourth repetition of this performance; broken only by a trip to the lavatory, the Lieutenant popped his earbuds out. "What are you doing, Sergeant?"

Rick uncapped the water bottle. "Well, the two biggest dangers with air travel are jet-lag and getting a clot in your leg because you didn't move enough, right? So, I looked up how to avoid those two things. With the clot, you just have to move every so often; with jet-lag, the top two tips I found were to sleep and stay hydrated."

The Lieutenant nodded. "Oh."

After a moment, he got up, returning shortly thereafter with a bottle of water.

***

As they disembarked, Rick squinted against the glare. Spotting Harry, he moved to join him as they fell in with the rest of the Engineers lining up. "Good to see you made it, Slim Jim."

Harry's eyes twinkled with quiet amusement at his nickname; a reference to his near-addiction level of fondness for Slim Jim snack sticks. "Very funny; Leslie said she would send me a box of them in the mail."

Rick smirked. "They won't make it if the Supply Sergeant figures out what they are. I should have given her one of my itching powder booby traps when I said goodbye."

Rolling his eyes at the mention of the custom-designed booby traps Rick had made, Harry turned to follow the line as they marched towards their barracks. "So, you think that Leslie bought the line we fed her?"

Rick shrugged. "The one about us heading to Africa for humanitarian support efforts?"

Removing his 'cover,' or hat, as they entered the barracks, Harry nodded. "Yeah. I kind of feel bad about lying to her, but that was the official line we were supposed to say."

Looking around, Rick gave a mental snort as he nodded agreement. While the place they had actually deployed was similar to Africa in that it was hot and dry, the similarities ended there. Whereas Africa was a rich continent of discovery and conquest, this land was a barren waste littered with the bones of explorers and would-be conquerors: Macedonian, British, Russian, and a hundred more, who had sought to add this small country to their empires, only to fail as those who had come before them had. Setting his duffel on his assigned bunk, he wondered if America would be added to the list of those who had sought to subdue Afghanistan, the graveyard of conquerors. *Well, technically we're not trying to subdue Afghanistan, per se; we're trying to help the locals kick Al-Qaeda and the Taliban out, so, theoretically, we're safe from ending up on* that *particular list.*

Chapter 3

The Fight Comes

The next day he was out repairing and strengthening the roads likely to be used by the up-scaled patrols, with an element of the Black Knights on security, and preparing the roads for the follow-on echelons: elements of the 1st and 2nd Marine Regiments, nicknamed 'Warlords' and 'Timberwolf', were due to arrive in a month to help reinforce the units already in place, and there were rumors that units of 'Gunslingers' and 'Iron Horse', the 2nd Divisions' artillery and tank support, respectively, were going to be moved over within two or three months. Operations in Afghanistan, and especially Kandahar Province, where they were deployed, had been getting more involved, and they needed the support.

The patrol security element leader, a scarred, placid-faced Lieutenant named Reynold Dawes, had served with the Black Knights in Phantom Fury, helping to drive a mixed bag of insurgents out of the Iraqi city of Fallujah in what was later described as some of the heaviest urban fighting US Marines had been in since the battle of Hue. In the course of the fighting, he had earned a Purple Heart and a Bronze Star with a V for rescuing six wounded members of his company from a burning LAV-25 while under intense enemy fire.

The roads had already been cleared of mines and IEDs, but several of the devices had damaged the roadways when they were blown up, and even when that had not happened the bridges were usually in no condition to support even an eighteen ton Stryker Infantry Fighting Vehicle, much less a seventy-two ton M1A2 Abrams main battle tank; on most of the bridges the fourteen-ton LAV-25 Armored Personnel Carriers were pushing it. Consequently, the Engineers were out to repair the damaged bridges, and make the others strong enough to support the tanks of 'Iron Horse' as well.

Late in the afternoon a week and a half later, as they were putting the finishing touches on a bridge repair job, Rick suddenly looked up at a ridge about one hundred yards away, where something was moving. Turning to one of the Marines from the 'Black Knights' security element, he pointed. "Possible contact—." He never finished the sentence, as a rocket blast tore the road three feet away from the LAV-25 the Marine was standing next to, showering it with shrapnel. "Hostiles on the ridge!" shouted the rifleman as the LAV gunner swiveled the cannon around and loosed off a thundering burst of fire, the 25mm high-explosive rounds shattering rock and kicking up huge gouts of dirt and dust as the rest of the patrol opened fire. Viciously berating himself for leaving his rifle in the vehicle, Rick dashed up the side of the riverbed and into the LAV, grabbing his M16A4 rifle and a dump pouch of magazines, snatching up an AT-4 disposable rocket launcher before scuttling out the back ramp and dashing behind the boxy LAV. Popping up, he searched for a target. Spotting a muzzle flash on the ridge, he fired a series of three-round bursts but only succeeded in ticking off one of the Taliban machine gunners, who unleashed a long burst in his personal direction. Dropping below the top deck of the LAV as bullets smashed into the thin armor like hail on a tin roof, Rick ejected his empty magazine, grabbing a fresh one out of his web vest and sliding it into the rifle.

Chapter 4

Battles Fought

Pushing the bolt release and taking a deep breath, he popped up over the LAV again, centering his scope on the muzzle flashes of the machine gun, which had sought out more compliant targets and was hammering a group of marines who had been trapped partially in the open. Carefully squeezing the trigger, Rick fired off ten rapid shots, and then switched targets, aiming at an RPG-armed Taliban silhouetted on the ridge. Three shots later, he had the satisfaction of watching the insurgent drop from view. Shifting back over to the machine gun nest, he fired eight more shots, then blinked in surprise as the nest vanished in a cloud of smoke and debris. A second later, he spotted the tracers from the chain gun on the LAV to his right, which had finally gotten on target and obliterated it with thirty High Explosive Incendiary-Tracer rounds. Transitioning to his AT-4, he fired at one of the two mortar teams, the rocket off by a good ten feet. Snarling a string of imprecations as he fired his remaining bullets at the mortar team, he dropped to the ground to reload. Curling into a ball as a mortar round from a second mortar team blasted the ground behind him, shell fragments and pieces of broken rock clanking on the rocks behind him and beating against the vehicle, he tugged the empty magazine loose, pulled a fresh one out of his web vest, and shoved it into the rifle. Scarcely had he hit the bolt release when the Platoon Sergeant, who had been conferring with the Lieutenant, grabbed his arm. "On your feet, Marine! You don't want to miss this!"

Rick was about to ask what he meant, when the air was split by an unearthly roar as an A-10 Thunderbolt II 'Warthog' swooped overhead, releasing a trio of Rockeye II cluster bombs and blanketing the ridge in bomblets that crackled and popped like a giant string of firecrackers, followed by a pair of Mk 77 incendiary bombs that bathed the area in a hellish glow. Amid the cheers from the Marines, Lieutenant Dawes rose from his position by the second

LAV's front set of wheels. "All right then, now that that's done with, all unit's report status."

It was soon discovered that two Marines were wounded, and one killed. Ordering a medevac chopper, Lieutenant Dawes turned to the rest of the patrol. "Okay, let's get back to work."

Nodding, Rick walked back to the bridge, muttering with annoyance to discover that either the Taliban had been deliberately targeting the bridge or had been badly off target, as three mortar rounds had impacted on a section of the span, destroying the approach slab nearest their side of the bridge and damaging the near-side piling. "We're going to have to replace the slab here, and either replace or repair the piling."

For the next three hours, they labored to remove the damaged slab and shore up the middle section so that they could check the piling. Finally, Lieutenant Dawes called a halt for the evening, and they headed back to base.

As they offloaded their gear in the barracks, Harry noticed Rick sitting on his bunk, staring at a picture of himself, Leslie, and Harry standing on the edge of the Grand Canyon. "Remember this trip? That was when I asked Leslie to be my girlfriend."

Grinning, Harry unslung his backpack, placing it at the foot of his bunk before coming over to look at the picture. "Oh, yeah. That was also when you tried to impress her with your driving skills and almost drove off the bridge, and then managed to make her think you were just testing the car's anti-collision software, right?"

Nodding, Rick chuckled. "What I couldn't believe was that she actually believed me. Of course, we mustn't forget what you did the next day, must we?"

Harry nodded innocently. "What, you mean finding that amazing little Mexican restaurant and treating everyone to lunch?"

Rick shook his head, smirking. "No, ordering the hottest salsa on the menu, loading a chip as full as you could, and then gagging so bad you squirted salsa out your nose an all over the waiter."

Harry rolled his eyes, shoving the heel of his hand into Rick's head and toppling him over onto the bunk before returning to his own bed to finish unpacking.

Chapter 5

They Are Back

Over the next five weeks, Rick's company managed to finish the job on that bridge and repair or replace three more bridges before being transferred to the construction of the school planned for one of the local villages. While the local headman of the village was in full support of the project, the Taliban presence in the area was less than thrilled at the idea and began intensifying their attacks against the Marines and the villagers, as well as attempting to destroy the school itself. Barely a week after the foundations had been laid and the walls had begun to rise, a chillingly accurate mortar strike leveled the fledgling structure and caused twenty casualties. Eight of them were Marines, three of whom died. A series of aggressive patrols and drone strikes combined with increased surveillance knocked out the worst of the raids, but the Taliban would not give up so easily.

***

As the unmistakable sound of incoming shells split the air, Rick dove for cover behind a pile of rubble cleared away from the previous attack. One hand clamped on his helmet, he waited out the three explosions and then popped his head over the pile to check for damage as the platoon leader's voice rang out. "Anyone hit?"

Rick glanced left, and right at the Marines he could see, all of whom were unhurt. "We're good over here!"

"Good to go!" The other Marines called out. Everyone waited tensely for further mortar rounds, but none came, just the thudding return fire from the three 120mm mortars that had been brought along as security. A quick check of the schoolhouse revealed that nothing had been damaged; this was the work of a 'shoot and scoot' team of insurgents trying to get a shot off but not willing to hold still long enough to be accurate.

Hearts at War

With sighs of relief, mixed with expressions of aggravation, the Engineers returned to the task at hand. This pattern of random mortar strikes had been going on for about a week now, but the next day, the insurgents changed tactics. It started the same way as always, with a trio of mortar rounds crashing randomly around the school building, but this time the rounds were followed fifteen minutes later by a blaze of machine-gun fire as forty Taliban insurgents broke cover and began to advance, firing on the Engineers and their security element as they came. From his position atop a ladder, nailing down part of the roof, Rick spotted the rocket team a heartbeat before an RPG came sizzling toward him. Eyes widening, he grabbed the outer edges of the ladder, kicked his feet out to grab the outside, and slid down the ladder, the rocket exploding where he had been a split-second earlier as he landed at the bottom and turned to run. Ears ringing in two off-key tones, he felt as if his eyes were being expelled from their sockets as he was pummeled into the ground by the blast wave. Digging his elbows into the ground on instinct as his mind fought for control of his discombobulated body, he began crawling behind a nearby stack of lumber intended for the roof framework, shaking his head hard to clear it. Rolling over onto his back as he got behind cover, he pushed his goggles up onto his helmet rim and shoved the heels of his palms into his tightly closed eyes to alleviate the sensation of their being popped out of their sockets. After a moment, as his hearing began to return and his mind reasserted full control, he grappled with his rifle briefly before bringing it around to the front of his body, peering out from behind the wood and searching for targets. He did not have to look far. Six rifle-armed insurgents were less than fifteen yards away, firing on full automatic at Marines hunkered down behind the corner of the schoolhouse. Out in the open, their focus on their targets, they made easy targets for Rick. Four of them fell to his fire, and the remaining two were taken out by a machine gun on one of the mortar vehicles. Scrambling over to the nearest LAV, Rick huddled for a moment, catching his breath as the cannon thundered over his head, cutting the Taliban charge to pieces.

With most of the hostiles in the open dead, the Marines began to shift their fire to the hills outside the town, where machine guns, rockets, and rifles still hammered the Engineers. A quick call to base confirmed that they were also under sustained and heavy attack; no help would be forthcoming from that quarter.

Chapter 6

Moving Forward

For twenty minutes the battle raged, with one of the LAVs being destroyed in the course of the fighting, and six more Marines killed and wounded. Finally, the attackers broke and ran, with mortar fire pounding after them. Wiping the sweat from his face, Rick flopped down against the rear wheel of the bullet-scarred LAV he had been hiding behind, carefully holding the hot rifle away from his body as he fumbled with his canteen. Leaning the rifle against the vehicle, he downed the entire quart canteen in long, gulping swallows. As he shook out the last drops onto his outstretched tongue, his platoon commander appeared, silhouetted against the glare of the sun. "How are you doing, Sergeant?"

Squinting his eyes against the light, Rick managed a weak grin. "Oo-Rah, Sir."

Nodding, the commander helped him to his feet. "That's the spirit, Marine. Let's take a look at what they've done to the schoolhouse."

The battle had taken its toll on the structure, with bullet holes and some blast damage, but all in all, it was much less than it could have been. Most of the exterior work would have to be redone, but fortunately, they had not yet begun putting in plumbing, much wiring, or detail work. As they waited for the new shipment of lumber, his platoon joined the work on the base fortifications: construction of new bunkers, repair of old ones that had been damaged in the fighting, building a new set of barracks and fighting holes for the projected troops due to arrive any day, as well as construction of fortified positions for the expected artillery and tanks. No sooner had they finished construction on the schoolhouse than his whole company was attached to the entire Black Knights company and two companies of Warlords Regiment to set up a Forward Operating Base eighty kilometers to the northeast. Their mission was to keep an eye on suspected terrorist activity believed to be responsible for the recent spate of attacks on Highway 1. As they bounced and rumbled along the miserable, rock-studded, broken excuse of a road leading to their base, Harry leaned over, raising his voice to compete with the roar of the massive engine. "This road is like the one we hit on that horrible bus tour we took out in the Rockies, remember?"

Rick groaned at the memory. "Don't remind me! That was the one where the tire blew, the rats had gotten to the spare, and they couldn't find the map, right?"

Nodding, Harry shook his head. "That was one of the worst experiences I have ever had on a bus tour in my *life*."

The rest of the trip was spent trying to get less uncomfortable; comfort was not a primary concern for the manufacturers of the LAV-25 Marine Fighting Vehicle and consisted of hard plastic benches with some vague attempt at seat-shaped in-dentations and crude padding. Arriving at the location of the base-to-be, they climbed somewhat stiffly out of the vehicles and headed over to the supply trucks, hauling out rolls of barbed and razor wire, Concertainers; the wire and heavy fabric collapsible cages that would be filled with earth and rock from the trenches to form semi-permanent fortifications for the base, fuel and water tanks, pallets of MREs; the Meal, Ready-to-Eat rations the military subsists on, and all the other paraphernalia required to keep the war machine of the Marines running.

Firing up a pair of front-loaders, the engineers began assembling the Concertainers and digging entrenchments. In about six hours they had the outer perimeter assembled, as well as most of the fighting holes, the beginnings of a Stores bunker, and two machine gun positions, and were putting the finishing touches on the mortar position. Final assembly of the barracks took another hour, and then they knocked off for the day. The next day, after completion of the helicopter landing pad, the Stores bunker, and the Command Post, or CP, basic construction on FOB "Mike Oscar" was complete. The company, along with the rest of the FOB garrison, would remain for the next two months and then return to Camp Henderson, the base they had been originally deployed to. The first four days were tranquil, but on the fifth day the patrol spotted a Taliban supply column and called down a strike from Firebase El Cid, one of the outlying 'Gunslingers' fire-bases. Backtracking the trail of the column, it was discovered that there was a group of villages under direct Taliban control that they were using as a base of operations for the area. The decision was made to eradicate the Taliban, and a strike force comprised of two platoons of 'Warlords' as the main strike force, and one of 'Black Knights' as recon were assembled. Riding once again with the Black Knights, this time as an embedded engineer along with Harry, Rick's job was to deny the enemy mobility out of the town once the battle was joined.

Chapter 7

Rolling Storms

Stopping their LAVs out of sight of the village just before sundown, the Marines made a final check of their gear. Emptying his pack, Rick sorted through his supplies: Claymore Mines, plastic explosive, detonators, insulated wire, fuzes, shock tubes, Det Cord, and initiating systems. Satisfied, he repacked and slung his pack, moving to join his assigned platoon as they prepared to advance to their blocking position. Having made a 'sound check,' each member of the team jumping up and down in place to see if there were any pieces of kit that made noise and securing anything that did, they set off at an easy jog, making for the far side of the village.

Reconnaissance had indicated that the Taliban had a concealed bolt-route out of the village leading to an almost invisible mountain pass that would give them an easily defensible avenue of escape; pocked with caves along its length, and extremely narrow in numerous places, it would make pursuit impossible at best, and suicidal at worst.

However, by placing a screen of the Black Knights across the roadway leading to the pass, they could either terminate any retreat or stall it long enough for friendly assets to neutralize all hostile presence in the area. His NVGs bathing the area in an unearthly green glow, Rick knelt to one side of the road, emplacing a pair of Clay-more Mines set at an angle to sweep the road, with one about twenty yards behind the other. Arming them, he set them to command detonation and then moved to the middle of the road, pulling out a small pick and shovel and hacking a trio of shallow holes in the packed earth. Pulling three directional shaped charges out of his pack, he settled them quickly in the holes, loosely covering them with earth before retiring to his position. Flipping off their NVGs to conserve battery, the team waited, watching the darkened buildings of the nearest village. After a few moments, a nearby Private scooted closer to Rick.

"So, why do the locals hate the Taliban so much? I mean, they claim to share the same faith and stuff, and we're the infidels, right? So why when we get to a village to help them and stuff, do they love us and hate the Taliban?"

Overhearing the question, the nearby fire team leader snorted. "Just wait until the Taliban walk into the village. Then it's, 'Kill America, Taliban good!' It's the same old story all over the world. Whoever's around waving guns, that's who the locals are going to support."

Rick shook his head. "That doesn't explain the Northern Alliances' cooperation with the Greenie Beanies back in 2001-and-2, or all the times that we get genuine tips from the locals about the whereabouts of Taliban positions and movements. To answer your question, Private, as far as I can tell, it's because the Taliban enforce a code of Islam that is a whole lot stricter than what your average Afghani Joe is happy with. They enforce pretty much the Koran to the letter, whereas most of these guys want to live a more normal/secular life, paying lip service to the tenets of Islam. That makes hard-core believers like the Taliban mad, so they come down like the proverbial ton of bricks on the locals. This in turn ticks off the locals, so they come to us for help, and we treat them nice most of the time, so they like us. I mean, think about it. If you had to choose between a group of guys who oppressed you, shot or stoned your women if they were educated or didn't wear a tent in public, cut the hands off of thieves, beat and imprisoned you and your family if they didn't have beards, and stuff like that; or a group of guys who built you schools and medical facilities, respected what you believed without trying to impose what they believed on you, helped you get food and housing, and protected you from the other guys whenever they could and went out of their way to kill those other guys, well, who would you like and try to help whenever you could?"

The platoon leader's voice cut off further conversation as it buzzed over the radios. "All right, look sharp. The main assault is due to kick off any minute."

After a minute of tense waiting, the deceptive calm of the night was suddenly torn by a series of sharp explosions and the harsh chatter of gunfire. The past two days of reconnaissance had, in addition to discovering the hidden pass, revealed the more or less exact locations of where the Taliban holed up in the area were bunking for the night; believing themselves more or less secure, they made little effort to change their sleeping arrangements on a night-to-night basis. Consequently, the assault teams had been able to pinpoint their objectives instead of fumbling around and having to kick in every house on the block to get their targets. From the sounds of things, the assault was progressing almost perfectly. They had opted for the 'shock and awe' option, blowing the doors and using flash-bang grenades to pacify the occupants.

As the battle moved inexorably forward, Rick felt a hand squeeze his shoulder twice, the signal to power up their NVGs again. Reaching back to acknowledge by tapping the hand once and then flipping his down, he reached out, grabbing Harry's shoulder and squeezing twice. As Harry tapped once to acknowledge and turned to pass the signal on to the next man, Rick turned his attention to the roadway ahead, scanning for the first sign of movement that would betray a hostile advance. Finally, he heard the muffled reverberations of engines floating through the darkness to his ears as five trucks came rumbling down the road toward them, clearly foregoing lights in an effort to be less conspicuous, although if they thought about it, a single drone with thermal imaging would tag them in a second. However, they didn't think about that, and came on at a slow but steady pace, obviously trying to balance speed with noise as they fled the battle which, it was obvious even from here, was tilting rapidly in favor of the Marines. Watching them get closer, Rick mentally calculated their approach. *Thirty meters…twenty meters…ten meters.*

Rob Winblad

Chapter 8

Worth The Fight

As the first truck rolled over the nearest shaped charge, he hit the trigger, slitting his eyes almost shut as the searing flash blanked out his NVGs for a second. A half-second later, Harry triggered the second and third, set further back but not far enough; the second just missing the second truck as the third clipped the engine block. As it stalled and swerved sideways, the third truck crashed into its' rear, the fourth truck stopping with minimal room to spare.

To either side of the road, in semi-fortified positions, the Marines opened fire with a combination of rifles, machine guns, and AT-4 and LAW-66 rocket launchers, along with a few hand grenades. The Taliban tried to put up a fight, but they were firing blind, in the open, with no idea who or where they were shooting, and it was all over in a matter of seconds after the first charge went off. Six of the passengers managed to duck into a small ditch to the left of the road, but that was where Harry had planted his Claymores, which he used to summarily dispatch them, and then it was all over. From the village beyond them, a few more gunshots rang out, and a LAV cannon fired off a short thundering burst, then silence reigned again, aside from the frightened sounds of civilians. Moving into the village, Rick joined a group of Marines talking with the village chief. Noticing a young child clinging to its mother's robe on the edge of the group, watching with round, unblinking eyes, he moved to crouch down in front of her, digging in his web vest for a sucker. Unwrapping it, he held it out with an encouraging smile. "Here. It's for you. Go ahead; take it."

Hesitantly, the little girl reached for the treat, her large dark eyes never leaving his face. His smile widening as she accepted it, putting it in her mouth, Rick rose to his feet, turning to rejoin his unit. With the village chief pacified, the Marines returned to their vehicles, satisfied with their night's work.

Chapter 9

Laying Traps

A week later, Rick and Harry were attached to a platoon of Marines from 'Warlords' on a clearing raid in another of the local villages. This time they would be part of the 'hammer' of the 'hammer and anvil' tactic; in this case the 2nd company of the 'Warlord' Marines. Jumping off just before dawn, they caught an element of Taliban in vehicles heading out of the village. Cannon fire accounted for the vehicles, and machine guns mopped up the survivors as they rolled forward without even slowing. As his LAV slowed, the hatch lowering to form a ramp, Rick moved in a crouching run to the side of the street, grimacing as shots rang out and bullets kicked up puffs of dust around his feet. Pulling his shotgun around, he fired a trio of shots at a window on the second story across the street where the shots had come from. Glancing back as he fed shells into his shotgun, he made sure that the rest of the platoon was dismounting and moving into position before following them to their first objective, a nondescript two-story structure with a simple wooden door. As the point man on the assault team knocked his clenched fist against his helmet, indicating 'breacher up,' Rick stepped forward, a Halligan bar in his fists. Setting the adze end of the tool between the door and the doorjamb with the bar pointed at the hinge side of the door, he nodded to Harry, who stepped forward as well, holding a shortened eight-pound sledgehammer in his grip; with a short ramming swing, he jammed the Halligan into the space between the door and the frame.

"Set," said Rick. Nodding acknowledgment, Harry moved out of the way as Rick stepped toward the handle side of the doorframe, levering the other end of the Halligan tool in the same direction and wrenching the door open.

As a spat of bullets chewed into the doorframe, the secondary pulled the pin on a flash-bang grenade and placed it in the outstretched hand of the point man, who released the spoon before lobbing it inside. In the wake of the flare of light and concussive sound, they began the entry. Gunshots rang out inside as the first two men in the door put down a trio of gunmen in the front room. Taking up the back of the line, Rick and Harry followed the last members of the assault team in; this wasn't a known multi-breach scenario, where one member would breach the outer entrance, and the other would breach the entrance to the main building, but they would follow the team in case they were needed further on. Transitioning to his primary weapon, a shortened Mossberg 500 shotgun, he listened tensely to the gun-fire, clenching his teeth in helpless rage as a pair of bleeding Marines were carried out.

Clearing the lower level without too much difficulty, the team moved to the staircase and began to climb, rifles moving with their eyes as they tried to cover all the angles at once. Halfway up, a grenade clattered on the stairs, rolling towards them. In a flash of motion, the point man snatched up the grenade, hurling it back up the stairs, where it hit the landing a second before it exploded, hurling fire and metal in all directions. From his position in the hallway across from the stairs, Rick didn't see what happened, but he did hear the grenade go off, and the ensuing gun-fire as the surviving insurgents on the second floor fought for control of the stair-well. Tapping the rearmost man on the shoulder, Rick placed his mouth close to the man's ear. "I'm going to see if I can get them from below."

Rob Winblad

Backing down the stairs as the man nodded, he moved to the room below the one where the insurgents were holed up, watching the floorboards flexing under their weight. Quietly bringing a chair over, he stood on it, placing the muzzle of his shotgun against the ceiling as he motioned to Harry, who was armed with an M4, to do the same. With a nod of comprehension, Harry stood under an area of the floor where several insurgents were clearly standing, clicking his rifle to full-auto. Holding up his left hand, Rick raised three fingers, bracing his shotgun against his shoulder. *Three. Two. One.* As his last finger came down into the fist, he pulled the trigger on the shotgun. The double-ought buckshot round contained twelve pellets, each one a fraction of an inch larger than a nine-millimeter bullet; smashing through the relatively thin planking of the floor, they ripped into the Taliban above him with murderous effect. The recoil threatened to knock him from his precarious perch, but he held his footing, racking another round in as he shifted his aim and fired again. Simultaneously, Harry triggered a long burst that ripped into the group above him, cartridge casings rattling and clinking on the floor around him. Racing up the stairs as six of the riflemen in the room were cut down, the assault team finished the job in a blaze of gunfire, then quickly cleared the rest of the upper floor, coming up empty. Regrouping in the street, they moved to the next objective, a pair of single-story buildings inside a walled courtyard. Testing the door, the point man shook his head. "Shotgun on me!"

Hearts at War

Walking quickly forward and pulling a breaching shotgun from his web vest, Rick waited until he passed the second man in the line before racking the slide to chamber a breaching round. Settling the muzzle in the doorway aimed at a 45-degree angle in and down, so as to shear off the bolt throw without endangering noncombatants on the other side of the door, Rick clicked the safety off and looked over at his 'cover man,' the one who would be first inside. As the cover man nodded, Rick fired, pivoting away from the door, his boot heel thrusting backwards into the door to knock it open as he moved rapidly away from the door, allowing the entry team access to the courtyard. At the back of the line, Harry followed them inside with his sledgehammer out and ready. Scattered gunshots rang out in the courtyard as the entry team engaged hostiles both in the courtyard itself and in an upper room of the main building. Securing the courtyard and chasing the hostiles in the window to cover with several long bursts of fire from the SAW, they gathered by the door. "Sledgehammer up!"

Running forward, Harry 'choked up' on the sledgehammer handle, coiling his body into a ready position. "Set."

"Go!"

Uncoiling, Harry slammed the hammerhead into the door, popping it open and swiveling away to withdraw at a forty-five-degree angle from the entry team. Another flash-bang preceded the entry team, as Rick waited in the courtyard; out of the line of sight of the upper window. A moment later, Harry joined him, settling down in the meagre shade afforded by the wall. "Not much we can do here. It's pretty much a bunch of open connecting rooms; some half-walls, some dead ends, but other than that, no real structural surprises."

Watching as the first of the flex-cuffed and blindfolded prisoners began to be marched out, Rick nodded silent agreement, tilting his canteen and taking a long drink. Finally, the call to regroup went out, and he got to his feet, giving Harry a hand up before they moved to rejoin the platoon. Remounting the LAVs, they were about to head for the main rally point when an urgent call came over the radio. "Warlord Two Actual this is Warlord Papa Five Leader. We are pinned down in the old fortress, requesting backup; repeat, we are pinned down and need backup, how copy, over?"

Chapter 10

Fight Another Day

After a brief pause, Captain Blake, the leader of 2nd Company, responded. "This is Warlord Two Actual, solid copy, Papa Five. Warlord Papa Two, you're closest to the fortress. Move to reinforce Warlord Papa Five; how copy, over?"

Keying his radio, the leader of their platoon spoke.

"This is Warlord Papa Two, solid copy, Warlord Two Actual. Warlord Papa Two is on its way, out."

Turning the channel to the intra-platoon network, he continued. "All Warlord Papa Victors, make for the old fortress to back up Warlord Papa Five, how copy, over?"

As the rest of the platoon's squad leaders acknowledged, the six-vehicle convoy raced for the old fortress, an imposing structure set in the middle of the town; up on a slight rise, it had been giving some of the assault sections trouble with mortar fire, which had finally petered out as the lower level was taken. Rolling through the shell-shattered main gates, the LAVs came to a halt in a cloud of dust as their back ramps opened to disgorge the Marines, who began to run for the next doorway. The fortress was built with a large outer courtyard that had contained the now-deceased mortar teams as well as several fighting pits, broken by an inner wall that contained the main 'keep'; essentially a large multi-roomed bunker that led into a labyrinth of tunnels beneath the fortress. Running through the bunker door, they began clearing it one room at a time, coming to the tunnel network. Taking a deep breath, the platoon leader turned to the rest of the men. "All right. Two men behind me, and then a breacher. Second breacher hits the back of the line. Ready? Let's go!"

Rick was about to take his place fourth in the line when he felt a hand on his shoulder. "Let me do it," said Harry. Shaking his head, Rick moved into position. "Not this time."

Moving forward at a fast walk, their lights slicing through the dust and darkness, the platoon headed into the tunnel. After twenty seconds of walking, they heard the sound of gunfire and picked up the pace. Suddenly turning left, the platoon leader entered a side room that turned out to have two Taliban fighters trying to bandage a third, who had been wounded by shrapnel. Looking up as the intense white light from the flashlights cut through the gentler yellow glow of a lamp that lit the room, the first one opened his mouth to yell, then shut it abruptly as he spotted the rifles pointed in his direction and the other men moving in. *"Get on the ground! Get on the ground! Do it now!"* commanded the Lieutenant in a low, harsh voice. As the two men obeyed immediately, he continued without taking his gaze from them. "Felix, cuff 'em."

Moving forward, careful not to compromise the fields of fire of the three men covering the prisoners, Corporal Felix Boyd pulled out two pairs of flex-cuffs, cinching them tight enough that they were secure without cutting off blood flow or causing nerve damage. "Secure."

Sitting the two men against the wall, the Lieutenant shoved his pistol into the more frightened-looking man's face, nodding to a shadowed tunnel entrance at the back of the room. "All right. Where does that go?"

Clearly, in a panic, the man babbled in Pashtun for a few seconds before managing a string of broken English. "Slit tunnel-go around-other way-no kill!"

Backing up, the Lieutenant holstered his pistol and re-gripped his assault rifle, moving down the tunnel at one step below a run. Less than thirty feet down, the tunnel broadened into a large cavern with several tunnels and small caves branching off of it. The platoon originally sent to clear the fortress had become pinned down in one of the side caves; raked by hostile guns, they struggled to return fire, both sides skittish of using grenades or rockets underground. Coming out largely behind the main Taliban position, Rick's platoon fanned out and opened fire, catching their foes off-guard and tilting the balance immediately in their favor. Squeezing off single shots as he advanced, Rick noticed one of the hostiles pulling out a trigger device. "*Bomb*!" he shouted, centering his sights on the hostile's forehead and pulling the trigger twice. Both shots landed perfectly on target, sending the hostile crashing to the ground with his fist clenched around the trigger, but the device intact. Collapsing to the ground as the fighting came to a halt, the last of the Taliban having been killed, Rick took a deep breath as he contemplated the suicide bomber in front of him.

In the open it would have been devastating; underground, it would have been catastrophic, likely collapsing the chamber they were in as well as other pieces of the tunnel network, consequently sealing any survivors in and burying them alive.

"Idiot. Flipping idiot. Some of his guys might have gotten out alive if they had shot their way out, but who in their right mind brings a suicide vest underground?"

Surveying the aftermath of the battle, Harry shook his head. "A fanatic who wants an insurance policy if things go sideways. Let's get out of here."

Upon their return to the ground level of the fortress, the two platoons discovered that the rest of the fight had finished, and the town was secure.

Three weeks of relative calm later, Rick and Harry were called into the base's briefing room, which had been constructed three days after the night raid on the Taliban's base of operations. "Two days ago, a CIA drone pass picked up footage of a site they have been monitoring for a while in the Maiwand District, which on later inspection was decided to contain imagery of a high-ranking Al Qaeda operative, who, it is hoped, will help lead us to Bin Laden. You will be attached to the strike team as breachers. Any questions?"

Silence greeted the query, and the briefing officer nodded. "Good. Now, obviously, we don't have the resources for a full-scale rehearsal, but a table-map scale model has been constructed. You leave tomorrow at oh-five-hundred."

Clearing his throat, the assault team leader raised his hand. "Why so time sensitive, Sir?"

The base commander gestured at the satellite imagery still on the projector. "Because, according to the CIA analysis, this site is a flexible location for operatives; basically, it's like a layover point or a temporary safe house. Our target is not expected to stay long, so we need to move fast and capture him before he drops off the radar again."

As heads nodded around the room, he continued. "All right then. The model is in the next room. Good luck, gentlemen."

Moving into the next room, the assault team, a full-strength rifle platoon of Marines from 'Timberwolf', and Rick and Harry as the breaching team, gathered around the table, which contained a crude model of the house; a two-story building with a twenty-foot wall creating a courtyard with about thirty or forty feet between the wall and the building. In the courtyard were various pieces of litter: a half-dozen oil drums filled with dirt and rubbish, two or three piles of rubble and large chunks of concrete and broken rock, and a pair of derelict trucks. Gathering the tokens set out to represent the team, the Lieutenant began arranging them.

"All right. First Breacher blows the door, then Corporal Hanes will make entry with Private Ames and Private Crenshaw, followed by Second Breacher and the rest of the team. Inside the courtyard, we will suppress or terminate any opposition, and Second Breacher will blow the front door. Once we have gained entrance to the main building, we move to secure our target; with that accomplished, we will signal the extraction helicopters, and get out of there."

After settling the minor details, they spent the next five hours running a rehearsal as best they could with what they had.

Chapter 11

The Coming Doom

At oh-five-hundred, after making a final
check of their gear, they headed out to the
helicopters that would take them to the target; a
CH-53E Super Stallion transport for the strike
force, with a pair of AH-1W 'Super Cobra' attack
helicopters flying escort. Touching down out of
sight of the compound, which was located at the
edge of a fairly large village about twelve

kilometers east of the border with Helmand Province, they disembarked quickly, did a gear check, and began to travel three grueling kilometers to the target. Pausing just below the crest of the final ridge before the village to catch their breath, they surreptitiously glassed the compound. "Everything looks okay. No overt signs of increased security, at least since that Predator went over. Final gear check."

As they went over their gear one last time before moving down to the compound, Lieutenant Matthews looked at Rick. "Sergeant Newman, I meant to ask you this earlier; it's a little late to change things now, but why are you carrying an AT-4?"

Rick shrugged. "I don't know. It's almost like a superstition with me; I always carry one when I'm out on a mission, even something like a humanitarian op. Most of the time I don't need it, but I always have one."

The Lieutenant mulled that over for a moment and then nodded. "Okay. Hope you don't have to use it this time."

As he walked away to check on the rest of the men, Harry came over to Rick. "I know we never really nailed the order down, but I'd like to do the inner breach. That cool with you?"

After thinking about it for a moment, Rick shrugged and nodded. "Sure, why not?"

Rising to his feet, he banged fists with Harry and then walked over to his place in the line. Moving out at a brisk trot, the team made their way down the mountainside to the main entrance.

Unslinging his pack, Rick pulled out a small shaped charge pre-made to destroy the door's lock; attaching it to the lock, he taped a circular 'platter charge' to the center of the door; this would blow the door straight down after the lock was blown. Crimping Det Cord to the detonators, he inserted them into the charges, reeling the cord back around the corner. "Breacher has control." Announced the team leader. "I have control." acknowledged Rick, raising the fuze igniter. "Fire in the hole!"

As he gave the igniter a quarter turn, the twin fuzes set off, blowing the charges milliseconds later. The blast worked perfectly, flattening the door, and the assault team charged inside. Private Gardener, the third man behind Harry, had barely cleared the doorway when the point man went down in a spray of blood as bullets struck him in the face and neck.

Rob Winblad

Chapter 12

Losses of War

Watching from the side of the doorway, Rick's eyes widened behind his goggles as the point man went down, and he turned to the Lieutenant. But before he could call 'man down,' the Lieutenant was already rushing through the doorway; no sooner had he gained the courtyard, however, when bullets knocked him to the ground, blood welling from a wound in his side. Firing a long burst from his SAW at the window from whence the shots had come, Private Gardener drove the shooters to cover, whereupon Privates Crenshaw and Ames ran out and dragged Corporal Hanes and Lieutenant Matthews to cover. Hanes was obviously dead, but Matthews was still alive, face creased in pain as he clenched his hands over the wound, which had skipped under the body armor and glanced off of his hip bone before coming out into his backplate. Out in the gateway, Rick fired his entire magazine in three-round bursts at the hostiles visible in the windows and doorway of the building. Ducking for cover as a pair of rifles blasted at the gate, he reloaded, then unslung an AT-4 he had brought along. Raising it to his shoulder, he looked over at one of the other men, who nodded.

"Backblast is clear, backblast is clear!"

Stepping into the open, Rick sighted quickly on the upper window, where a machine gun had joined the riflemen firing at the Marines in the courtyard. With a whoosh, the rocket leaped from the tube to smash directly into the window, turning it into a ghastly hole of fire and death. Under cover of the explosion, Rick cast aside the empty launcher, unslung his rifle, and dashed into the courtyard, laying down fire to suppress the hostiles and cover his advance. As he dived behind a pile of rubble, however, fiery pain slashed through his right leg just above the knee. Crashing to the ground as the fire in his direction intensified, he half-rose and fired off his remaining rounds, then dropped back behind the rubble and reloaded before pulling out his pressure dressing and struggling to tie it to the ugly bullet wound in the muscle of his leg. Miraculously, it had missed both the knee joint just below, and the femur to the left, and had gone through the outside of the leg, thus missing the femoral artery, but it still hurt like liquid fire, and the pain was making focusing difficult. Sudden movement to his left caught his eye, and he looked up to see Harry crouched behind one of the derelict trucks, blasting away at the hostiles. Spotting Rick's predicament, Harry rose to a half-crouch, motioning to the man at his side and saying something that, while Rick couldn't hear, was chillingly clear.

"Harry, stay back! I'm good!" shouted Rick, knowing that Harry was asking for covering fire while he ran to Rick's position. But Harry either didn't hear or didn't care, and so Private Crenshaw laid down covering fire while he dashed into the open. Bullets immediately cut the air around him, chopping divots in the dusty ground, but he never slowed, until a burst of fire caught him in the back and neck, some rounds punching through the body armor, others punching a hole in his throat. Stumbling, like a runner who has caught his foot in an unexpected hole, he managed a few more staggering steps before his legs buckled and he crashed to the ground. His bandage forgotten, Rick jumped to his feet and tried to run to Harry's assistance, but his own leg gave way almost immediately, and he was reduced to crawling forward, grabbing Harry's harness and painfully dragging him back to cover. Under covering fire from the survivors inside, the rest of the team made it into the courtyard, suppressing the hostiles and shooting the door open. Agonizing minutes of gunfire followed, then a long silence. Finally, they emerged again, pushing a hooded and zip-cuffed figure before them.

A grim smile of triumph lighting his pain-streaked face, Lieutenant Matthews keyed his radio to the aircraft frequency. "Rattlesnake Five, Rattlesnake Five, this is Timberwolf Papa Eight Actual. The package is secure, we have three KIA and five casualties; I repeat, three Kilo-India-Alpha, and five casualties. Requesting evac, how copy, over?"

"Timberwolf Papa Eight Actual, this is Rattlesnake Five. Good copy, we are inbound, on your position three mikes, out."

Seven minutes later, Rick was strapped to a stretcher in a helicopter, with an IV tube in his arm and a Navy Corpsman crouched next to his stretcher applying a second bandage to his leg. From his position on the next stretcher over, Lieutenant Matthews gave him a thumbs up. "Oo-rah, Sergeant! Mission accomplished!"

Returning the thumbs up half-heartedly, Rick allowed his thoughts to wander. *Mission accomplished. We got a guy who may or may not help lead us to Bin Laden, and along the way one of my best friends gets reduced from a person to just another KIA. All because I had to go and let him in there first, and then get shot and not warn him off in time!*

Chapter 13

Come Home

Three Weeks Later:

Wearing his full Marine dress blues, Rick silently raged at his wounded leg as he was wheeled down the aisle and into a space in the third row of the outdoor funeral service. Sensing his inner turmoil, the Navy Corpsman who had volunteered to assist him leaned over from his seat to Rick's left. "Stay strong, Sergeant. None of this is your fault."

Watching Leslie sitting in the front row with her father and Sam and Annie O'Dooley, Rick silently disagreed. In his mind, he replayed the scenario again, as he had a thousand times before, coming to the same conclusion as always. *If I had gone in there instead of Harry, or if I had managed to wave him off, he would still be alive right now, giving me a hard time about getting shot so I wouldn't have to dance with Leslie and remind us all what a horrible dancer I am, or something like that.* Watching helplessly as Leslie broke down when the flag that had draped Harry's coffin was presented to her, Rick clenched his teeth in rage as the lonely notes of Fanfare for the Common Man sounded in the hot, humid air. As the funeral service ended, and the attendees began offering their condolences, the Corpsman wheeled Rick forward. As Mr. Wakowski turned around, he spotted Rick, a mixture of relief and concern crossing his face as he hurried forward. "Rick, good to see you! How bad is it?"

Uncomfortable at the concern, Rick shrugged. "Not too bad. The doctors said that in a couple of weeks I should be able to be on my feet again. Thanks."

Annie ran forward to take his hand. "Hey, Rick! I'm sorry you got shot; does it hurt much?"

As Rick nodded, his eyes tracking beyond Annie's shoulder, she was about to say something else when she noticed where he was looking and stopped, rising to her feet and backing up. Her eyes red and swollen, Leslie looked briefly down at him, nodding. "Hello, Rick."

His heart sinking at her tone, Rick tried to keep his voice steady as he replied. "Leslie, I'm so sorry. I—"

Her own voice at the breaking point of grief, Leslie cut him off. "Rick, please; not now. Some other time, okay?"

Slumping back in his wheelchair as her words appeared to confirm what he had hoped to deny, Rick swallowed back his apology unsaid and motioned wordlessly for the Corpsman to take him back to the car. *You were right. She knows that it's better off without you, and she decided to let you know that discreetly rather than publicly break up with you.*

Over the next few weeks, he struggled to keep up with the physical therapist's goals, performing the required tasks out of sheer stubbornness. Noticing his attitude, one of resigned grit rather than optimistic determination, and mistaking it for despondency over his injury, the therapist took him aside after one of his last sessions. "Look, Sergeant, you took a hit, but it's not as bad as it could have been. I mean, you could have died out there, or lost limbs, but you didn't, and you can come back from it."

Rick nodded, not meeting her eyes. "I know; thanks for the pep talk, Doc, but save it for someone who is giving you problems, okay? I'm good."

The therapist appeared ready to continue, but he forestalled further comment by grabbing his cane and limping for the exit, and she abandoned the subject with a sigh. Finally, five frustrating and tense weeks later, he was finished with the therapy, and after moving into a modest rental home, headed over to Wakowski Construction. As he walked in, Trudy looked up with a smile. "Hi, Rick! I haven't seen you in a while. What can I do for you?"

Shrugging, Rick sat down. "Well, I was kind of hoping that Mr. Wakowski might have a job opening that I could apply for."

Nodding, Trudy shuffled through a stack of files. "Yes, as a matter of fact, there is an opening on the framing crew, if you're interested."

Trying to keep the relief from showing, Rick nodded. "Absolutely. I don't really have much to keep me occupied right now since I got a medical discharge from the Marines with my leg, and I'm kind of looking for a way to pay the bills if you know what I mean; plus, I really wanted to find something local."

Accepting the application form, he filled it out on the spot, bid Trudy good day, and drove back to his new house. He had enough squirreled away from his pay to keep him afloat for two months, but he wanted to keep that as an emergency, and the job at the construction company would cover his expenses nicely and leave him with a little left over. Two days later, he got the call he had been waiting for. "Hi Rick, it's Trudy. We have reviewed your application and would like you to come in for an interview. Would tomorrow at 2:00 p.m. work for you?"

"Yes, that would be great. Thanks, Trudy."

The interview went well, and within a week, he had started work. As he came home from his fifth day on the job, he found a letter in his mailbox from Leslie. Half hopeful that she had changed her mind, half fearful that she had not, he sat down at the kitchen table to read it.

Rick,

I can no longer continue our relationship after what happened. While I do not know all of the particulars, I am sure that learning them would prove too painful and knowing would not bring my brother back to life. Please consider this our last communication, and do not attempt to contact me again.

Leslie.

For a long moment, he sat hunched over the table, staring down at the note, his heart sinking into a cold, empty place as he read the final nail in the coffin of his guilt; the bang of the judge's gavel as it were, sealing his doom as Harry's killer. Dropping it on the other end of the table, he dragged himself up to his room, where he sat on the edge of the bed for a long time with his head in his hands as the voices of self-recrimination and censure, which he had managed to fight for the last two months with varying degrees of success, poured out their invective on his head, more savage than anything another person could have come up with, railing at him for his crime. Finally, as they faded, for the time being, he prepared for bed and tried to sleep.

Chapter 14

Time Keeps Moving

Five Months Later:

The heat of the sun, beating down on his back. The choking dust of the scorched and barren ground on which he lay, straining his eyes through the smoke and confusion. The searing pain in his leg as he crawled toward the still form ahead of him; a dark trail of blood smeared in his wake. The face of the man brutally clear, agonized eyes open in shock, blood dripping in a thin rivulet from his half-open mouth.

"Harry, no!"

His eyes snapped open, and he sat bolt upright, sweat streaming down his face as the echoes of the dream faded. Using the collar of his t-shirt to wipe the sweat away, he rose and walked over to the window, staring out at the drenching rain hammering the glass. A crackling flash of lightning etched the flooded yard for an instant, thunder rattling the house like a bomb blast, and he flinched. *Eight months.* Turning away from the window, his beleaguered gaze fell on the picture sitting on the dresser. In the photo, he stood on a pier with his arm around Leslie, her hair blowing in the wind as the setting sun bathed their smiling faces in a reddish-orange glow. Grimacing as a fresh stab of pain hit him, he crossed to the picture; a small part of his mind noting that the limp was almost completely gone as he picked up the frame, cradling it in his hands. "Oh, Leslie. Why did you have to fall for a weak loser like me?"

On a sudden impulse, he opened the top drawer of his dresser, shoving the picture to the farthest reaches of the drawer and slamming it shut.

As he turned to head back to bed, his alarm buzzed, announcing the official beginning to his day. With a sigh, he padded over and silenced the alarm, pulling on his shoes and heading downstairs.

After breakfast, he headed for his car, a dented blue Jeep Compass, sipping his coffee as he wove through the morning traffic. The job did not offer much, but it allowed him long hours and hard labor, both of which combined to exhaust him sufficiently that he usually slept through the night; although this morning proved that the past could still return to haunt him. Arriving at the construction site, he reported to the site overseer to receive his assignment for the day.

***

Three Weeks Later:

The psychiatrist's face said it all as she shuffled the papers on her desk. "Look, Mr. Newman, this is your eighth session; and so far, you have made a frustratingly low amount of progress."

From his position on the couch, Rick turned his head to look over at the psychiatrist. "Frustrating for you, don't you mean? I don't have anything else to talk about, but you seem to think that there is some kind of deep, dark secret that is inhibiting my life, and I need to reveal it to you in order to survive; or at least to be able to live a full, 'happy' life."

He paused, shifting back to stare at the ceiling. "Did I leave anything out?"

A short pause followed, then the psychiatrist spoke. "This kind of attitude is exactly what I am attempting to address. Your defensive obsession with denying the facts is leading to outbursts of sarcastic language and insulting behavior; this situation is leading to an increased antisocial outlook and withdrawal from the world around you. This pattern will ultimately lead to suicidal tendencies that, barring outside intervention, will eventually form into action. I am trying to prevent that from happening, but I can't help you if you don't help me and open up." Without ceasing his inspection of the ceiling, Rick replied. "And now we come to it. By 'help me and open up', you mean 'pour out my deepest, darkest secrets that may or may not exist, and co-operate when you manufacture fake conflict with various family members when I was too young to argue with your so-called professional opinion, and charge way too much money to leave me feeling bad about my childhood and indebted to you; and then feel good about what you've just done.' No thanks, Doc; I don't buy into that kind of garbage, thank you very much."

As he rolled off the couch and came to his feet, the psychiatrist scribbled more notes on the paper on her desk, her voice frosty. "Well, it is clear from your remarks that I can be of no further use to you. Therefore, this session is over, and all further appointments are canceled. If you want someone to unload your emotional filth on, go find a more gullible therapist to insult and abuse. Good day, Mr. New-man."

Heading for the door, Rick turned, his hand on the doorknob. "Translation: you're mad that I saw through your smoke screen to the vicious little brat hiding inside that lab coat."

Leaving the psychiatrist speechless with rage, he walked out, shutting the door behind him. *Stupid, Sergeant Newman,* he could almost hear Lieutenant Svenson, his former Engineers platoon commander, admonishing him. *That kind of confrontational attitude is why you have and likely never will advance beyond your current rank.* Suddenly a shadow seemed to pass before his eyes, and Lieutenant Svenson's smiling, exasperated features changed, becoming dust-caked and smeared with sweat and blood as they morphed into the tense, pain-streaked face of Lieutenant Matthews. *His eyes widened behind the goggles as the point man went down, and he turned to the Lieutenant. But before he could call 'man down,' the Lieutenant was already rushing through the gate; no sooner had he gained the courtyard, however, when bullets knocked him to the ground, blood welling from a wound in his side, just below the body armor.* Shaking his head savagely to clear the visions from his mind, he climbed into his car and checked his phone. A text from his site boss telling him that he was needed the next day on the development they were working on was the only new message, and after acknowledging, he deleted it.

The nightmares chose to spare him, and he slept soundly until dawn, when he arose, taking a bagel in the car on his way to the construction site. He was on the framing crew, and they were assembling the floor on the house that day. Reporting the site overseer, he soon found himself crouched next to the crawl space wall, holding the boards of the outer sill as his mates on the work crew screwed them together; with the sill completed, he grabbed a drill and began attaching the joists. The work passed quickly, and almost before he knew it the second wall was up, and it was time to knock off for the day. Heading home, he pulled a box of leftover take-out out of the fridge and ate at the small kitchen table as he continued reading the same book, he had been trying to read for the last two months. Finding himself re-reading the same page for the fourth time, he gave up with a sigh; reaching for a bookmark, he stopped as he realized that it was the break-up note from Leslie. Almost against his will, he scanned the shaky, blotted words. His hands shaking as the words burned themselves once again into his brain, he tasted blood as he bit his lip, a single tear tracking its way down his cheek. With a sudden wrench, he tore the letter to pieces, flinging the torn scraps of paper in the trash can, and trudged upstairs, pursued by the voices in his head: *Some soldier you were. Couldn't even keep him alive. Leslie was right to dump you, you know; how could she have ever loved you when every moment you were together reminded her of Harry; especially if she ever learned the truth about how he died? That you killed him? Get a grip, Rick! She's better off without you!*

Collapsing onto the bed with a groan, Rick clenched his hands to his head as he tried to shut out the voices, to no avail; he couldn't fight their logic, and he knew what they said to be true. As the accusing voices faded, he closed his eyes, knowing that sleep at this point would be difficult at best; but exhaustion proved more powerful than guilt.

Rob Winblad

Chapter 15

Inner Demons

One Month Later:

His eyes snapped open as he stared at the ceiling, trying to figure out what had awoken him. Suddenly something hit his window with a sharp tap, and he sat up, staring at the window. Without warning, there was a crash of breaking glass as something came hurtling through the window, and he rolled to the opposite side of the bed from the window, diving for cover behind the bed. Opening his mouth to equalize pressure from the expected blast and thus prevent his eardrums from rupturing, he wrapped his arms around his head as he lay flat on the floor and waited for the explosion. When nothing happened, he counted to fifteen before carefully looking over the side of the bed, then walking around to the other side, grabbing a flashlight from the bedside table, and bending down to inspect the offending object; a fist-sized rock. Walking carefully through the shards of glass littering his floor, he peered down into the yard, shining the flashlight through the broken window. His breath caught in his throat as he recognized the woman standing in his front yard.

"Leslie?! What on earth are you doing here? And why did you just put a rock through my window?"

Looking slightly sheepish, Leslie dropped the rock she held in her hand. "Well, I knocked, but you didn't answer, and your phone was either dead or turned off, so I decided to try to get your attention the old-fashioned way."

Shaking his head to clear the cobwebs, Rick hesitated for a moment. "Um, I thought that was usually the *boyfriend* who threw little pebbles at his girlfriend's window to get her attention."

Leslie shrugged. "Well, I guess that turns the tradition on its head. Look, I'm sorry I woke you up, and I'm really sorry that I broke your window, but can we talk?"

More than a little suspicious, but nonetheless acquiescent, Rick headed downstairs and unlocked the door, waving her inside. "Sure, come on in; can I get you some coffee?"

Shaking her head, Leslie looked around at the front hall, her expression tense. With a shrug of his own, Rick led the way into the kitchen, indicating a chair. "Please, sit down."

As she seated herself, he started his coffeemaker, preparing a pot of coffee. "Sorry, I just can't really think too straight right now, seeing as how I was kind of asleep five minutes ago."

With a nod, Leslie waited while he set the controls and put away the can of grounds, then sat down at the table. "Okay, what did you want to talk about that was so important that, after you said you never wanted to talk to me again, you came to my house in the middle of the night, and heaved a rock through my window?"

Looking uncomfortable, Leslie fidgeted with her hands, first looking at the tabletop, then at the painting of a harbor with a schooner-rigged ship at anchor hanging on the wall, then back at the tabletop. "I wanted to ask you about what happened when my brother died."

Rick felt like he had been punched in the throat; rocking back in his seat, he stared at her, his voice a susurrous rasp. *"What? Why?"*

Leslie's face reflected the pain she obviously felt at having to ask, but she persisted, her own voice wobbly. "I have to know. Rick, for eight months I've been trying to put my life back together, and as I've been thinking more and more about it, I realized that I had been completely unfair to you as well as to me by breaking up the way that I did, and for that I am truly sorry."

Clearing his throat, Rick tried to speak, failed, and tried again. "I forgive you, Leslie. But believe me, you don't want to know what happened that day. It still gives me nightmares."

Leslie closed her eyes for a moment, then opened them again, staring at Rick and making eye contact for the first time in the conversation. "Please, Rick. I have to know. Not knowing what exactly happened has been pure torture; the unknown is a chapter of my life that I can't close until I find out what happened."

For a long, long moment Rick sat very still, concentrating on breathing as the voices in his head lashed him with their rancor, then he nodded. "All right. I'll tell you. It was in Kandahar Province, twelve klicks—"

"I'm sorry, 'klicks?'" asked Leslie.

"Slang for kilometers. Anyway, twelve klicks east of the Kandahar-Helmand border. We had received word of an Al-Qaeda operative holed up in a compound located in the Maiwand District, and Harry and I were attached to the strike team to perform the breach. We didn't have the time or the resources to perform the normal rehearsals; all we had was a couple hours on a model of the target building."

He paused as the coffeemaker beeped at him. Pulling a mug out of the cupboard, he poured the coffee and returned to his seat at the table before continuing. "We jumped off at five in the morning, getting to the compound two hours after dawn. As we were making the approach, Harry pulled me aside and convinced me to let him take the inner demo spot while I blew the outer gates. At the time I couldn't see a reason why he shouldn't; the compound was supposed to be lightly defended, and the rest of the team would be right behind him to take down any unexpected threats. I blew the main gate; a textbook breach, nothing I hadn't done a thousand times before, just vanilla-plain C4 and Detonating Cord. The only problem was that surveillance had underestimated the number of security that the target had with him; instead of twelve or thirteen fighters, there were between thirty and forty. As we were making entry, the point man and the Lieutenant went down, and we were pinned down in the gateway; the point man, Lieutenant, Harry, and three others were inside, and everyone else was outside. The point man was dead, the Lieutenant was only wounded, and the other three had managed to get to cover and bring him with them. I had an AT-4 with me and blew out an upper story window that was housing most of the active shooters as well as a machine gun; under that cover, I made a break through the gate, but as I was running through the gate, I took a bullet in the leg. As I was making my way behind cover, I spotted your brother. He was about fifteen feet away behind an old truck. He saw me trying to bandage my leg with bullets chopping all around me, and he broke cover to come help me. But as he was running across the open ground, he got hit in the back and neck multiple times. One of the other guys gave me covering fire, and I managed to drag him back to the wall I had been sheltering behind, but by that time it was too late. Harry was dead; I killed him."

Closing his eyes, he waited silently for Leslie to affirm what he knew, to pour forth her censure and anger for what he had done, and to leave once and for all. Instead, he felt a gentle hand on his arm and heard her voice, gentle and soft. "Rick, what are you talking about?"

Opening his eyes, he stared at her, his face raw. "Don't you understand? I should have been the one in the courtyard!

If I hadn't let Harry talk me into letting him take secondary, he would have been safe outside, and I would have been the one inside! If I hadn't gotten hit, he wouldn't have broken cover and gotten killed!"

Moving to sit beside him, Leslie wrapped an arm around his shoulders, pulling him close. "Rick, stop, don't talk like that. You couldn't possibly have known how it was going to play out; you didn't deliberately send Harry in there to get killed, and you didn't deliberately get yourself shot so that he would break cover and get killed. Harry would have done that for anyone of his team members; there is absolutely nothing for you to blame yourself for. From what you've told me, you saved a lot of those men by shooting the window out and stopping the bad guys' machine gun."

Rick tried to believe her, but the voices in his head would not abate; continuing to accuse him of being a coward, a fool, and utterly unworthy of her. Unaware of the battle raging in his mind, Leslie continued. "The other thing I wanted to talk about was, well, us. I was an idiot to cut you off the way I did, and I was wondering if you would be willing to give me another shot at our relationship."

Panic washing over him like a tidal wave, Rick fought to keep from hyperventilating as the two conflicting portions of his thoughts battled for control; on the one side, emotion cried out that not only did Leslie deserve a second chance, but he did as well, that she had forgiven him, and he needed to accept her offer; while on the other side, reason spat back that someone as cowardly and despicable as he would never be worthy of her, and therefore he could under no circumstances accept her offer. As she stared at him with a mixture of hope and expectancy, he swallowed hard and spoke. "Um, I need to think about that for a while. Is that okay?"

Looking slightly hurt, Leslie nodded. "Of course, if that's what you need, sure. Good night."

At the door, she turned. "I will be praying for you, Rick. Never forget that."

Rob Winblad

Chapter 16

Save Yourself

As the door closed, Rick took a deep breath and surrendered to reason. There was no way he could allow Leslie to be hurt by him again; but with what she was saying now, there was no way she would understand that he was doing it to protect her. Returning to the kitchen table, he grabbed a piece of paper and a pen, and hastily scribbled a note:

Rob Winblad

Dear Leslie,

I know that what I am doing may seem very painful to you, but I want you to know that I am doing this to protect you. I am going away, and I don't know if I am ever going to be able to come back. Please do not feel obligated to wait for me; someone far more worthy of you will undoubtedly come along and make your life complete. Do both of us a favor by erasing me from your mind and allowing the better man to give you happiness.

Signed,

Rick

Setting the pen down, he walked over to the cabinet where he kept his correspondence materials, selecting an envelope and stamp. Returning to the table, he carefully folded the page, sliding it into the envelope, which he then addressed and set in his mailbox before climbing up the stairs to his room. Staring at the broken glass littering his floor, he shook his head. *Deal with that in the morning.* The next day was his day off, and he slept late. When he arose, the first thing he did was to clean the glass up and call a window replacement service. That done, he methodically set about pulling up his stakes in the area: First, he notified his boss of his two weeks' notice, then mailed his landlord the keys to the house and next month's rent. That done, he notified the post office of his impending absence, and, finally, packed his bags. It did not take particularly long; the house had come fully furnished, and his day-by-day existence over the past eight months had not been conducive to acquiring a great deal of personal possessions. Loading his bags into the car, he looked back one final time at the house and then drove away. Away from this house, and the memories it contained. Away from his job, and the friends who knew nothing of who he really was. Away from Leslie, and the false hope that he might someday be worthy of her.

As he merged into traffic on the Interstate, he allowed himself to think. *Where to go from here? Where can I run that is far enough away that Leslie will be safe while still being realistic?* Pulling off at the next rest stop, he consulted a road map of the United States that he had in the glove box, finally deciding on Arizona.

***

Two Weeks Later:

Climbing back into his car, Rick allowed himself a small smile for the first time in a week and a half. He had driven for five days to get to Arizona, staying at a string of cheap motels he had not even bothered to check the names of; arriving, he had booked a week in advance and begun looking for a job. It hadn't been easy, but he had finally found an advertisement requesting a driver for a local armored car service. The interview had not gone as well as he had hoped, but in the end, his military service and the fact that there were no other applicants had landed him the job. He would start in three days, and while the pay wasn't as good as some of the jobs he had applied for in the past, it was fairly high on the security job pay grade. Unfolding the newspaper on the seat next to him, he flipped over to the housing section, finding an entry he had circled two days previously. **Two-Bedroom One Bathroom Studio Apartment. Fully Furnished.** Pulling out his cell phone, he dialed the number in the advertisement. After five rings, it connected. "Hello, this is Rhiannon Daniels."

"Hello Mrs. Daniels, my name is Rick Newman, and I was wondering if I could arrange a meeting to discuss renting the studio apartment listed here in the paper."

"Sure. Tomorrow at - uh, say ten? - at the apartment?"

"Perfect. Ten o'clock a.m., correct?"

He could almost hear the smile on the woman's face as she replied. "Yeah. See ya tomorrow."

***

Pulling up in front of the apartment, Rick surveyed the exterior; non-descript but clean, it looked promising. Checking his watch, he climbed out, walked up the short concrete sidewalk, and hesitated briefly before knocking on the neat, green front door. A moment later it was opened to reveal a short, thin, gray-haired woman who inspected him for a moment through her small round glasses before nodding. "Mr. Newman? I'm Rhiannon. Come on in, I'll show ya 'round."

Following her inside, he walked through a narrow hallway with a door leading off of it, and then up a set of stairs to the studio apartment. As advertised, it was fully furnished, with a Zoku loft-style layout. After the walkthrough, he nodded. "I'll take it."

Chapter 17

Pages from The Past

Riding shotgun in the armored car, Rick unfastened his seat belt as they pulled up in front of the store. Hopping out, he walked quickly inside, nodding a greeting to the clerk. "Morning Clancy."

Returning the nod, the clerk pulled the cash box out. "Morning Rick."

Signing for the money, Rick quickly carried it to the car, breathing a sigh of relief as he locked the door. It was short-lived, however. As he was coming around the corner of the truck, two men in ski masks ran toward him, guns drawn. "Hands up, sucker! Now open the back!"

Holding his ground, Rick raised his hands, watching them carefully. Inpatient with his lack of movement, the taller of the two thugs shoved his pistol into Rick's face. "Hey! This is a real gun, fool! I ain't jokin', now open the stupid door!"

Rick's hands moved in a blur as he ripped the pistol from the thug's hand. The rules had been clear in his training: *use of force only permitted in genuinely threatening situations, lethal force only authorized if you are in danger of losing your life.* That definitely applied in this situation, but he didn't want their blood on his hands, not to mention the hassle of paperwork that their deaths would generate. Gripping the pistol by the slide frame and trigger guard, he punched the magazine/handgrip into the taller thug's throat, just above the top of the sternum. As he fell to his knees clutching at his throat, Rick kicked him into his companion, knocking him off-balance. Securing the gun in his left hand, he pulled out his baton and clubbed the second thug across the right shoulder as he began to raise his own gun, knocking him to the ground as the pistol dropped from his nerveless fingers. Standing back from the pair, he got on the radio to his partner. "Kevin, get on the phone and notify the police, and then notify the bank of our delayed arrival."

Looking down at the two men lying on the ground, the one wheezing for breath as he twitched feebly, the other sobbing like a baby as he tried not to move his broken shoulder, he sighed. *My second week on the job, and already I have to file an incident report.* The next few minutes were spent waving off passersby and waiting for the police to arrive. Finally, the sound of sirens announced their arrival, and then a police cruiser came screaming onto the scene.   Hopping out, the first officer had his service pistol out and trained on the two suspects almost before his feet touched the ground. Resisting the urge to roll his eyes, Rick waved him off. "Relax, Officer. They're both down."

As the officer, who was both young and clearly new on the beat, held his position, the driver, an older man with short-cropped graying hair and eyes that had seen it all, climbed out and walked around to the passenger side, placing his hand on the younger man's pistol and pushing it to point at the ground. "He's right. Holster your weapon and radio it in while I handcuff 'em."

Reluctantly, the younger officer obeyed, and his partner began to handcuff the two men, advising them of their rights. As backup arrived, Rick told his side of the story, and the suspect with the broken shoulder was transferred to an ambulance. After briefly interviewing several bystanders, the older officer walked over to Rick. "I'll need you to come down to the station and make a statement, but it looks pretty open and shut. We have several witnesses who back up your story."

He paused, then looked over at Rick. "From what they say, you didn't panic with that gun in your face, and you showed some pretty slick moves. Where'd you see action, Iraq?"

Brow furrowing, Rick looked back at him. "What makes you think that I was in the military?"

The officer shrugged. "Mostly the fact that while you didn't panic, your name doesn't show up in any police databases as a former officer. Most people with a piece trying to pick their nose for 'em wet their pants or start screaming, but witnesses we talked with so far say, you stayed as cool as a snow-cone; so I figured you'd been in combat before."

Rick nodded, his eyes on the man being placed in the back of the police cruiser as his mind went back to the moment when the thug shoved the gun in his face. "You're partly right. It was Afghanistan."

After making his statement at the police station the next day, Rick found himself riding shotgun again, this time on a jewelry run. Forcing himself to relax as he relived the events of the previous day, he shook his head. *Cut it out! The cops were chill about it, you didn't kill anyone, and the boss was fine, so stop worrying!*

Noticing his discomfort, Kevin grunted sympathetically. "Jitters finally catching up to ya? It took, like, thirty seconds for me to start shakin'. Yer a cool one when it's on, though, I'll give ya that." Rick shrugged. "There are worse things than dying that can happen to a man. And no, it's not that; I was just running over my statement at the police station; they seemed pretty chill about the whole thing."

Nodding, Kevin braked for a red light. "Well, they got a lot of run-ins with us over the last five, six years. Robbin' banks doesn't pay so hot, so the locals have started robbin' armored cars. Sometimes, yeah, they get away with it, other times we're holdin' 'em, or, well, yeah, they're dead. Then the cops get called in, so they're used to us."

The rest of the drive was spent in silence, each man lost in his own thoughts. As they stopped outside the jewelry store, Rick was struck with a sudden impulse and wrote down the address. The following week on his day off, he went to the store, looking over the jewelry. As he walked over to the next counter, a beautiful diamond ring caught his attention. The week before shipping out the last time to Afghanistan, he had bought Leslie a ring for her birthday, and in consequence, he had her ring size in his phone. Driven by forces he could not explain, he checked the ring, finding that it was exactly her size. Looking up at the clerk, he gave a mental sigh. "I'll take it."

As he walked out to his car, he looked at the bag, wondering what had come over him. *You know you're never going to see her again, and you will never be worthy of her hand. What are you going to do, send her boyfriend this ring and expect him to use it?*

Trying to ignore the accusing voices in his head that bombarded him with similar sarcastic soliloquies, he drove back to his apartment, stowing the ring with his few possessions.

Chapter 18

The Only One

Two weeks later:

Setting the bag of groceries on the cheap linoleum table in his kitchen, Rick began to sort them, putting the non-perishable items aside and immediately moving the perishables to the small refrigerator. Turning at a sound behind him, he squinted against the morning sun at the figure in the doorway of the kitchen. "Oh, good morning Mrs. Daniels."

As his landlady smiled a return greeting, he sighed patiently. "Um, Mrs. Daniels, you've forgotten to put your dentures in again."

With an apologetic and entirely toothless grin, Rhiannon turned and walked back downstairs to get her false teeth. Returning his attention to the refrigerator, Rick shut it quickly. He was paying most of the utility bill and had no interest in allowing the scorching Arizona temperature add another fifty dollars to his bill that month because he decided to stare at the inside of the fridge for another minute and a half ruminating about which empty shelf to put the milk on.

As he walked the few feet to the table and began gathering up the boxes and jars of groceries to put in the cupboard, Rhiannon returned, this time with her false teeth safely in place, and poured herself a cup of coffee. Closing the cupboard, Rick put two pieces of toast down and stood by the window staring out at the barren landscape. As he watched the flight of a small bird from the porch to a bush, he found himself inexplicably struck by memories of him and Leslie, something that had not happened in over a month. Frowning, he thoughtfully drummed his fingers on the counter as he cogitated the reason behind the memories of a girl he had effectively erased from his life as a protection measure for her. *Is it because she needs you? Impossible! And yet, she could think she . . . Oh shut up; you're not psychic!* But he could not shake the feeling that something was wrong with his 'Run away, get as far away from her as you can, and she will be safe from you, to move on, to find the perfect man, and live happily ever after' master plan. The sound of his toast popping up shook him out of his reverie, and he quickly prepared breakfast, and then headed for work, trying hard to shut out the doubts and second-guesses that plagued him. As he brushed by Rhiannon, she watched him go with a thoughtful expression as she contemplated the inner turmoil so obvious on his face, a look she had seen several times now and was seeing more and more as the days went by.

As he returned from work the next day, he found Rhiannon sitting in his living room/kitchen area, her ever-present cup of coffee cradled in her wrinkled hands. "Siddown, Rick. We gotta talk."

Eyebrows rising in surprise, Rick obeyed, pulling a chair over from the kitchen. "Okay; what's wrong? Did I miss the rent or something?"

Shaking her head, Rhiannon set her coffee cup on the table. "No. It's about why you're here. I didn't ask what brought'cha out to Arizona when ya first started rentin' from me. But I just can't shake the feelin' that you're runnin' from somethin', er someone? Son, it's tearin' ya up."

Rick was silent for a moment, his mind racing through various possibilities of how this conversation could go, then spoke. "Okay, so assuming that you're right, what relevance does that have on our current situation?"

Rhiannon took a sip of coffee before replying, settling the cup back on the table. "The 'relevance,' as ya say it, is: I need ta know what you're runnin' from; I won't shelter a criminal on the lam, an' I won't help ya hide from your family."

Rick looked relieved. "Oh, well if that's all, then I can assure you I am neither on the run from the law nor fleeing my family. I . . ." His voice trailed off as he thought about why he had run. Watching his face, Rhiannon offered no comment, merely sat silently waiting. Part of Rick's mind protested that she had no business knowing his story, but the other part of his mind welcomed the opportunity to unload the burden he bore to someone who clearly offered neither judgment nor condemnation; someone who had already seen so much that nothing he could say would shock her. "I *am* on the run, but it's to protect this girl I know."

Rhiannon listened quietly as half-willingly, compelled by an impulse he could not explain, he poured out the whole story: the mission in Maiwand, Harry's death, Leslie's break up and subsequent visit, her forgiveness and desire to try again. "I can never be worthy of her, and Harry's ghost will always be hanging over our relationship; so, I told her that I needed time and space to think about it and ran."

For a long moment, silence reigned in the room, and then Rhiannon got up and refilled her coffee cup, pouring him one as well. Returning to her seat, she looked at him.

"Harry's ghost'll only hang over your relationship if yer holdin' on to it. Sounds ta me like Leslie's figured out how ta grieve, how ta let go; but yer trapped! That guilt 'n blame your holdin' makes ya think ya gotta cut yourself off from your old life. Ya think ya gotta be some outcast 'cause Harry got killed. That's not true. No, it's just not true. Ya gotta forgive yourself, son. Ya gotta move forward. Ya didn't kill Harry, son. Ya didn't put the Al-Qaeda fighters there to kill him, 'n wound you, 'n kill the other men. Forgiving yourself, Rick: it's the hardest kind of forgiveness, but if ya don't want to spend the rest of your life runnin' from somethin' ya never had ta run from, to begin with, ya have to forgive yourself."

Rick's eyes were as bitter as the coffee before him as he replied. "You have no idea what you're talking about. You've never had something like this happen to you, so stop lecturing me about something that you have never even come close to feeling, okay?"

Rhiannon got up, heading for the stairs to her house. "I've come a lot closer'n you think, boy."

As she walked down the stairs, her voice floated back to him. "Don't go away, I'll be back."

For several minutes, Rick sat in silence, waiting; then, just as he was about to leave, footsteps sounded on the stairs again, and Rhiannon made her way back up the stairs with a box in her hands. Setting it on the table next to her coffee cup, she carefully lifted off the lid, placing it to one side. The first thing she pulled out was an old framed photo of a man wearing an Army dress uniform clearly standing for a posed shot, with an American flag in the background. He stared out at the viewer with calm resolve, his expression calm and determined. "This is Carl. He was my husband."

After examining the photo, Rick handed it back. "What happened to him?"

Rhiannon sorted through a stack of correspondence, coming up with an official-looking letter with the US Army seal on the letterhead. "I think ya should read this. You'll see."

Nodding, Rick took the paper. It was clearly a form letter, sent out by the thousands to the next-of-kin:

Dear Mrs. Daniels.

It is with deepest regret that I inform you that your husband, Sergeant Carl Daniels, was Killed In Action on the twenty-first of October, nineteen sixty-eight, in the Giai Truong Son Highlands, the Republic of Vietnam.

Chapter 19

Birth of Hope

The rest of the letter was political talk about how he died a hero serving his country, how he would be remembered as a patriot and cetera. Looking up, Rick shrugged, confused. "I still don't see how this changes anything."

Rhiannon closed her eyes for a moment, then took off her glasses and polished them. "All right, yeah. See, I was a war bride, back in 'sixty-six;

Carl and I were married day before he shipped out for 'Nam. I wrote him letters, 'most ev'ry week. 'Course, he only wrote back, like, once a month or so. In his letters, he told me 'bout a friend he'd met over there, Mark Kentworthy. I almost felt like I'd met him."

Rhiannon paused to take a sip from her coffee mug, more to regain her composure than to actually enjoy the harsh, black brew, and then carefully resettled her mug on the coaster before continuing.

"In October nineteen sixty-eight, I didn't get a letter. I wanted ta think he was busy, but he always wrote once a month, sometimes more, for two years. I started worryin'. Then, in December, there was no letter again. Lieutenant Kentworthy showed up with that — " she waved at the letter in Rick's hands. "He'd convinced the War Office to let him take it to me personally. He told me his story, so I'd understand. He'd been out on patrol with Carl and Charlie jumped 'em. They were pinned down for a day and a half before they could fight their way to a Landing Zone that the helicopters could use. When they were gettin' on the helicopters, a grenade landed near them. My husband threw himself on it before anybody else could. He died to save those men. Lieutenant Kentworthy blamed himself for Carl's death just like your blamin' yourself for your buddy's death. He was so broke up; claimed he should've jumped on it before Carl."

Her voice trailed off for a moment as she drew a breath, then continued.

"It was one of the hardest things I've ever gone through. I told Mark Carl's death wasn't his fault. He didn't throw the grenade, and he had to forgive himself, stop blaming himself for Carl's death."

She stopped, rubbing her eyes, then looked across at Rick. "So, ya see, I do understand what you're goin' through. If you'd traded places with Harry, he would've had to tell Leslie that you were dead, and I can tell you, that's at least as hard as losing a brother. Maybe worse. Now, before you ask, I can say that because I lost a brother in the war; he was a Thunderchief pilot shot down over Hanoi just off of Thud Ridge."

Her voice became softer. "Rick, ya need to forgive yourself, not only for yourself but for Leslie. If you keep running, she won't just've lost Harry, she'll have lost you, and it *will* be your fault that she lost you."

Rick sat in silence for a long, long moment, then nodded. "You're right. I can't do this to Leslie."

Standing up, he extended his hand to Rhiannon. "Thank you, Mrs. Daniels. Thank you for renting to me, but most importantly, thank you for helping me to see the truth, and for helping me to find the courage to forgive myself and stop running."

With a smile, Rhiannon rose to her feet, repacking the box. "You're very welcome, young man. Now, don't you worry about the rest of this month's rent. Go give that young lady a second chance."

***

One Week Later:

Rick took a deep breath as he pushed open the door to his old construction job's main office. He had had little difficulty securing his old rental house; it had been unoccupied, and the landlord had taken him back with no questions asked, but he wasn't so sure returning to his old job would be quite so easy. Looking up at the sound of the bell, the receptionist's eyes widened as she recognized him. "Rick? What on earth are you doing back here?"

Mistaking her tone of voice for disapproval, Rick swallowed. "Um, I was hoping to see Mr. Wakowski; if it's convenient. I — "

"Yes, yes of course! I'll tell him you're here!"

Pressing the buzzer, she spoke. "Mr. Wakowski, there's someone to see you."

Anton Wakowski did not sound the least bit pleased by the news. "Trudy, I gave explicit orders not to be disturbed. What about that is irrelevant to this particular situation?"

Trudy smiled. "Because it's Rick Newman, sir. He wants to see you."

There was a long pause, then Mr. Wakowski spoke, his voice marginally more congenial. "Show him in at once."

With another smile, this one directed at Rick, Trudy waved him ahead. "Go on in."

His heart in his mouth, Rick walked over to the door, opening it and knocking on the doorframe. "Mr. Wakowski, sir?"

"Come in, Rick, sit down! What is it you wanted to see me about?

Swallowing, Rick sat down. "Well, sir, for starters, I wanted to apologize for the abrupt manner in which I left your employment. That was unfair to you, and I am sorry for it."

Mr. Wakowski nodded, his narrow, pale face inscrutable. "I forgive you, and you're right, it was unfair to me; we've been rather short-handed for the past couple of months. Care to explain why you ran out on us the way that you did?"

Fighting the urge to swallow again, Rick nodded. "Well, long story short, I was running away from some personal issues, but I have come to terms with them. That brings me to the second thing I wanted to talk about. I was wondering, hoping really, that there might be an opening in my old framing crew?"

Mr. Wakowski was silent for a moment. "You're asking for a job? After the way you ran out?"

Rick wiped his sweaty palms on his pant legs as discreetly as he could and nodded. "Um, yes, sir, I am."

Mr. Wakowski pursed his lips. "Well, unfortunately, we have no openings on your old framing crew. With no idea how long you would be gone, or if you were ever coming back, we had to fill the gap."

Trying to hide his disappointment, Rick stood. "Understood; thank you for seeing me, sir."

Mr. Wakowski held up a hand. "Now hold on a minute, I wasn't finished. As I said, we haven't got any openings in the framing crew, but Bart got promoted last week to Manager, and, well, that left a bit of a hole in the region of site overseer. It would take some training, but it comes with better hours and a jump in pay grade. If you're willing, I'd be happy to just forget the last two months happened and hire you on as our new site overseer."

For a moment, Rick could hardly believe his ears, then he grasped Mr. Wakowski's outstretched hand in both of his, shaking it heartily. "Yes, sir! Thank you so much, sir!"

Nodding, Anton gave a small smile. "All right then, if you're through trying to make off with my hand, we'll get the paperwork filled out, and you can start your training on Monday."

As he left, Trudy gave him a thumbs up. "Welcome home, Rick."

Chapter 20

The Beginning

Climbing into his car, Rick took a deep breath. The last stop he had to make would be both his easiest, and his most difficult one of all. Pulling out his cell phone, he dialed the number from memory, waiting through the rings as he tried to control his breathing. Finally, she picked up.

"Hello?"

For a second, he sat with his mouth open and nothing coming out, then he cleared his throat and tried again. "Um, hi Leslie, it's Rick."

Leslie's voice betrayed a mixture of anxiety and relief. "Oh! Hi Rick; um, how're you doing?"

He hoped his voice didn't sound as shaky as he felt as he replied, "I'm doing good, I-I mean 'well'; how about you?" Silently he beat his palm against his forehead at how lame that sounded as he waited for her response; which, fortunately for him, was not long in coming. "I'm doing well. I've missed you."

"Um, me too. Listen, I was wondering if you'd like to get together for coffee? There's some stuff that I'd like to talk about if you're okay with that."

Leslie was silent for a moment. "Um, yeah, sure thing. Say, thirty minutes at the coffee shop?"

"Yeah, sounds great. See you there."

Hanging up, Rick drove to the coffee shop, the same place he had been employed before his enlistment in the Marines. Getting a table on the patio, he signaled to the waiter; a short college kid working a summer job at the cafe. "Hi, could I speak to the owner please?"

Clearly misunderstanding Rick's intent, the kid paled. "Listen mister, you haven't been here long enough for me to do something to you, but whatever it is, I'll make it up to you! Don't get me in trouble with the owner, please; I need this job!"

Rick shook his head. "It isn't you, I just need to speak to the manager; I, well, I'm an old friend, and I need to ask a favor."

Relaxing, the waiter showed him to a table on the patio before making his way swiftly inside and returning a few moments later with the owner. Rising, Rick extended his hand. "Mr. O'Dooley! Good to see you again, sir!"

Sam wrapped Rick in a bear hug. "Sure, and I haven't seen you since you lit out for Africa, Ricky me boy! Love of the shamrock, the Marines aged you, lad! Sit down, sit down. Now, what is it you wanted to talk to me about?"

Rick grimaced as he fiddled with hisfingers. "Well, you see, I wasn't actually in Africa; that was the official line we were told to tell people. My unit was actually deployed to Afghanistan — "

Sam broke in. "Wait a moment, you were over in Afghanistan when all that terrible fighting was going on over there?"

Rick nodded. "Yes; my unit was probably in some of that 'terrible fighting.' Anyway, while I was over there, some stuff happened that I can't really talk about, but during the operation Leslie's brother Harry got killed."

Nodding sympathetically, Sam interrupted again. "Aye, 'twas a hard time over here when we got that news. Only thing that kept Miss Leslie together was the news that you survived by the grace of God."

Rick cleared his throat. "I know, I talked with her a little bit at the funeral. You didn't see me, and that's okay; you were kind of tied up helping console Leslie and Annie. The problem was, I blamed myself for Harry's death, and consequently, I didn't feel like I could — wait a second, you said that she was glad that I survived? She broke up with me as soon as I got back Stateside!"

Sam shrugged. "What can I say, lad, women do daft things when they're grieving. Anyway, carry on."

"Um, right. I didn't feel like I could be in a relationship with her, so I was fine with our breakup. Okay, not 'fine,' but I felt like it was for the best. Then right before I pulled my vanishing act, she heaved a rock through my window and told me that she forgave me, and it wasn't my fault and that she wanted to try again. I panicked and told her that I needed time, then beat feet for Arizona where I've been living for the last couple of months. I thought that if I stayed away, she would forget about me, find the 'right' guy, and live happily ever after."

Sam looked disapproving. "So that's where you've been! Leslie's been worried sick about you, wondering if she drove you to do something desperate after what you told her about what happened over there, and the rest of us haven't had it too easy either! The last thing that she needed was for you to run for it, especially after she forgave you and told you that she wanted another go at you two being together! She told me last week that she wondered if you had stopped loving her, and that her asking for a second chance had pushed you to go find someone else. You should have just accepted her forgiveness, forgiven yourself, and given the two of you another go!"

Shifting uncomfortably in his seat, Rick nodded. "Yeah; I got the same kind of message from my landlady out in Arizona; that's why I'm here instead of still driving an armored car out in Casa Grande."

Clearing his throat again, he finally got to the point. "So, what I was hoping was that you could help me. I'm going to talk to Leslie in about," he checked his watch, "five minutes, maybe ten, depending on how the conversation goes, and I was wondering if you could keep the patio clear until we're through."

Nodding, Sam beckoned to the waiter. "Can do, lad. It won't be too hard; we haven't been crammed lately, but I'll have Trevor seat them inside."

As Rick rose to his feet, Sam clapped him on the shoulder. "Absolute best of luck, Ricky; and well done, coming back the way you did. That was brave of you lad."

With a smile of thanks, Rick waited, trying not to fidget as he watched the passers-by until finally, he spotted her walking up the street to the cafe, her face inscrutable behind the sunglasses she wore to combat the brilliant summer sun. Jumping to his feet, he met her at the door of the patio. "Hi, Leslie; thanks for meeting me like this."

With a small smile, Leslie shrugged, removing her sunglasses to reveal eyes shadowed with badly hidden pain. "Well, you asked nicely, and I didn't have any pressing appointments."

Pulling her seat out for her, he seated himself opposite her, the words that he had practiced again and again over the last week flying from his head as he looked at her face. After a few minutes of uncomfortable silence, Leslie spoke. "So, what was it you wanted to talk to me about?"

Fighting the urge to lick his suddenly dry lips, Rick sent up a silent prayer for the right words to say as he took a deep breath. "Well, when we last were together, I told you that I needed some space to think about what you had said; that you wanted to give 'us' another try. When I left, I was unable to forgive myself, and thought myself utterly unworthy of you; so, I ran for it, thinking that if I disappeared for long enough, the 'right guy' would show up, and you would finally be happy. But then I had a revelation: by running away and refusing to forgive myself, I was not only destroying my life but also yours; you were losing not only your brother but me as well."

Biting her lip, Leslie nodded, two tears beginning a shiny track down her cheek. Reaching across the table to take her hands in his, Rick continued. "When I realized this, I knew that I had to forgive myself, release the guilt of the past, and come back to you to give us a second chance. I know I don't deserve it, but would you give me a chance to start over, and try again?"

As Leslie nodded again, he rose to his feet, releasing her hands, and took a step back. "All right. Thanks a bunch."

Taking a step toward her, he extended his hand. "Hi, I'm Rick Newman. What's your name?"

Rising to her feet, Leslie attempted a smile that mostly succeeded. "Pleased to meet you, Rick. I'm Leslie Nichols."

Rob Winblad

Epilogue

Beginnings and Love

Eleven Months Later:

"Dearly beloved, we are gathered here to bear witness to the marriage of this man and this woman. Marriage is the holiest of sacred covenants, an earthly representation of our eventual union with the Son of God in eternity. It is time now for the exchange of vows, the terms of this blessed and binding contract."

Turning to Rick, the pastor continued. "Do you, Richard Thomas Newman, take this woman to be your lawfully wedded wife, to love and to cherish, to guard and to honor, in sickness and in health, for better or worse, for richer or for poorer, to have and to hold, so long as you both shall live?"

"I do."

"And do you, Leslie Anne Nichols, take this man to be your lawfully wedded husband, to love and to cherish, to obey and to honor, in sickness and in health, for better or for worse, for richer or for poorer, to have and to hold, so long as you both shall live?"

"I do."

The pastor smiled as he gestured to the groomsman, who stepped forward and handed over the rings. "It is now time for the exchange of rings. In the shape of the ring, we see a circle, a symbol of eternity and a representation of the unbreakable and everlasting nature of your vows to each other."

Accepting the ring from his groomsman, Rick slid the ring onto Leslie's finger. "With this ring, I thee wed."

Leslie took his hand, her eyes sparkling as she slid the ring onto his finger. "With this ring, I thee wed."

As the pastor turned them to face the assembled guests, Rick caught Rhiannon's eye, smiling slightly as she nodded approval. Oblivious to the silent communication, the pastor continued. "By the power vested in me by the State of South Carolina, I now pronounce you man and wife. What God has joined, let not man rend asunder."

After a brief pause, he finished. "You may kiss the bride."